"*Surely* you don't believe in fairies?" Sarah-Jane shrugged. "Some grown-ups believe in fairies. It says so in my book. And lots of people believe in angels and things . . ."

Joe looked at Alice. Alice did not meet his eye. Then he looked at Mum. "Mum! Tell them there's no such thing as fairies!"

Mum, who was stacking things in the dishwasher, laughed. "Who knows, Joe?"

Joe slammed his spoon down. Had the world gone mad? "I know! *I* know there's no such thing as fairies!"

YOUNG CORGI BOOKS

Young Corgi books are perfect when you are looking for great books to read on your own. They are full of exciting stories and entertaining pictures. There are funny books, scary books, spine-tingling stories and mysterious ones. Whatever your interests you'll find something in Young Corgi to suit you: from families to football, from animals to ghosts. The books are written by some of the most famous and popular of today's children's authors, and by some of the best new talents, too.

Whether you read one chapter a night, or devour the whole book in one sitting, you'll love Young Corgi books. The more you read, the more you'll want to read!

Other Young Corgi books by
Emily Smith to get your teeth into
PATRICK THE PARTY-HATER
ANNIE AND THE ALIENS
ROBOMUM
THE SHRIMP
ASTRID, THE AU PAIR FROM OUTER SPACE

Joe v.
The Fairies

Emily Smith

Illustrated by Georgie Birkett

YOUNG CORGI

JOE V. THE FAIRIES
A YOUNG CORGI BOOK : 9780552559041

Published in Great Britain by Corgi Books,
an imprint of Random House Children's Books

This edition published 2005

Set in 17/21pt Bembo Schoolbook by
Falcon Oast Graphic Art Ltd

Young Corgi Books are published by Random House Children's Books,
61–63 Uxbridge Road, London W5 5SA,
A Random House Group Company.

Addresses for companies within The Random House Group Limited
can be found at: www.randomhouse.co.uk/offices.htm.

THE RANDOM HOUSE GROUP Limited Reg. No. 954009
www.kidsatrandomhouse.co.uk

A CIP catalogue record for this book is available from the British Library.

Printed and bound in Great Britain by
Cox & Wyman Ltd, Reading, Berkshire.

For my mother

One

Joe Campbell sat on his football
– and glared. Joe had a problem. It
was fairies. There were fairies in his
garden. They weren't just at the
bottom of his garden either. Oh, no.
They were all over the garden.
Dancing, skipping, singing – doing
all sorts of fairy stuff. It was enough
to make you sick!

Joe wobbled on his football.
Suddenly he saw the
three fairies skipping
towards him. The first
one was throwing
handfuls of pink
petals. The fairy
passed close by,
appearing not
to see him. But

a few of the petals she threw fell onto his bare knee. Joe brushed them off crossly. And lost his balance. And fell off his football.

Two

It all started when Cousin Sarah-Jane came to stay. Before she arrived Joe's sisters were . . . well, OK. Sometimes they were a pain, particularly little Rosie – but then she was little. Alice and Rosie never talked about fairies. Alice and Rosie never played fairies. As far as Joe knew they never even *thought* about fairies. And then Sarah-Jane came to stay.

Joe thought of the day she arrived. He and Alice and Rosie had spent the morning making an assault course. It was Joe's idea. They set it up to show Sarah-Jane what a lot of fun she was going to have at the Campbells'.

Sarah-Jane's family lived abroad and the three Campbells had only met her once, at a wedding. Joe and Alice could hardly remember her (and Rosie not at all).

They put a lot of work into that assault course. The climbing frame was the main bit. But you also had to balance on planks and jump over flower-pots and crawl under a sheet.

They timed themselves with Joe's new stop-watch. Joe's record was thirty-three seconds. Alice was just behind with thirty-eight seconds.

Rosie took nearly four minutes at first – she wasted a lot of time standing and arguing – but then got the hang of it, and got quicker every time (the rules weren't so strict for her). The all-time record, however – eighteen seconds – belonged to Bert, Rosie's hippo.

Sarah-Jane arrived with her mother just before lunch. The first impression Joe got of Sarah-Jane was of whiteness. She wore white trousers, a pink-and-white shirt, and clean white trainers. Very clean white trainers. But Joe wasn't too worried. You *did* look tidy at the beginning of a stay, didn't you?

The two mums did most of the talking at lunch (wholemeal pasta and tomato sauce). And very boring it was, too. But suddenly Sarah-Jane's mum was looking at her watch and talking about catching a plane and traffic to the airport. Then she kissed Sarah-Jane, and was gone.

The girls took Sarah-Jane and her big blue suitcase up to their room. And then the three young Campbells took their guest into the garden. The four of them stood and gazed at the assault course. It looked pretty good, Joe thought proudly. "You could have a go if you like," he said in a casual sort of way.

Sarah-Jane said nothing.

"It's quite easy, actually."

Sarah-Jane still said nothing.

"But not *that* easy."

Silence.

"I won't time you if you don't want."

Finally Sarah-Jane spoke. "No. I don't want to."

Joe looked at her, amazed. How

could anyone not want to go on their assault course? "Why *not*?"

Sarah-Jane screwed up her nose. "I don't *want* to crawl under a dirty old sheet or walk on planks. I don't see the point."

"She doesn't have to if she doesn't want to," said Alice.

Joe felt stung. Couldn't she at least *try* after all their work? "Well, if it's just your clothes—"

"It's *not* just my clothes!" said Sarah-Jane. "I don't like doing that sort of thing!" And then she did something that amazed Joe. She shot him a look of pure dislike . . .

There was silence again.

"Well," said Alice. "Shall we go upstairs and you can get your things unpacked?"

"You've got pink coat hangers," said Rosie. "Pink and squishy."

Sarah-Jane nodded. "OK." The three girls went back into the house.

And Joe, after kicking the grass for a bit, followed them in.

Three

The girls didn't look particularly pleased to see Joe when he went into their room. But they didn't tell him to get out either.

Sarah-Jane was sitting on the camp bed. And by her feet, open, was her big blue suitcase. Alice and Rosie were putting Sarah-Jane's clothes away in the two shelves they had cleared.

"Love this outfit!" said Alice, holding up something mauve.

"This one's all fluffy!" Rosie

15

stroked the front of a T-shirt. "Look, Bert!" she told her hippo, who was sitting on the bunk bed. "It's fluffy, like you!"

"You're so lucky!" said Alice. "You've got lovely clothes!"

"Mmm . . ." Suddenly Sarah-Jane looked mysterious. "And there's something else."

Her words hung in the air for a few seconds. And then she put her hand into her case and drew out . . . something white. And frothy. And sparkly. She held it up, twinkling in the light.

"Wow!" said Alice.

"It's beautiful!" breathed Rosie.

Even Joe was impressed.

"What is it?" said Alice. "A bridesmaid's dress?"

Sarah-Jane didn't say anything; she just turned the frothy white dress round, so they could see the back.

Rosie leaped to her feet and

pointed. "Wings!" she cried. And she
was right. They all gazed at the small
pair of gossamer-light wings fixed to
the back of the dress.

"I'd love to see you in it," said
Alice.

"You'd look like a real fairy!" said
Rosie.

"You think?" Sarah-Jane looked at
Alice sideways. "I know quite a lot
about fairies."

Rosie was still gazing at the dress.

"I've never been a fairy," she said slowly. "I've been a zebra and a cowboy and a pirate – except my eye fell off." Suddenly she looked indignant. "No, I've *never* been a fairy!"

"No," said Alice.

"Never been a fairy?" said Sarah-Jane. "Let's think . . ." She laid her dress carefully down and looked in her suitcase. "Yes, this might do!" And she pulled out a white nightie, with

white embroidery on it. "It would be a bit big for you, Rosie, but I don't think that would matter."

"*Yes!*" Rosie took the nightie, eyes glowing. "It's beau-tiful, Sarah-Jane!"

She turned excitedly to Alice. "And you could wear your bridesmaid's dress!"

Joe looked at Alice. Surely she wasn't going to go along with this? Little Rosie was one thing – but *Alice*? She wouldn't dream of dressing up as a fairy. Would she?

But there was a strange look on

Alice's face. "I could wear my ballet shoes," she said slowly.

"And tinsel! Tinsel would make us glittery like Sarah-Jane!" said Rosie.

"We'll need something for our hair," said Alice, going over to her chest of drawers. "Perhaps something flowery!"

"I'll go and look in the Christmas box!" said Rosie.

Suddenly Joe could be silent no longer. "But what about *me*?" he cried.

Three faces looked at him. Sarah-Jane gave a little frown. "What do you mean – 'what about you'?"

"Well, I can't dress up all pretty, and play fairies! What am *I* going to do?"

For a moment there was silence, and then Joe thought he saw a sudden glint in Sarah-Jane's eye.

"Perhaps you could be a gnome!" she said.

"*What?*"

"Yes!"

Sarah-Jane

gave him a wide smile. "You could be a gnome and carry my tiara round on a cushion!"

That was when Joe stormed out.

Four

The fairies fairied all the rest of the
day. Dancing. Singing. Doing strange
things with flowers. Doing strange
things with leaves. Sometimes they
lay on the grass while Sarah-Jane
read to them out of a book about
fairies. She seemed very good at
thinking up fairy-type things to do.
The assault course was taken down,
and the climbing frame made into
something called a fairy bower.

Joe watched them grimly. The
summer holidays – and Sarah-Jane's
stay – were not going as he had
planned. He was worried too.
Suppose someone saw? Suppose word
got round that there were fairies
dancing around Joe Campbell's
garden? People would laugh

themselves silly!

Mum wasn't much help. The first time she saw the girls all dressed up, she said, "Goodness! What are you supposed to be?"

The fairies looked at each other. "What do you *think*, Mum?" said Alice.

Mum surveyed them. "Well, you could be princesses."

"With wings?" said Rosie.

"Angels, then."

"No!" said Rosie. "We're *fairies*!"

"Wow!" said Mum. "We have a band of fairies in the garden!" She looked at Joe. "Aren't we lucky, Joe?"

And Joe had no words . . .

At tea time, Alice put down her fork and frowned. "You know Mum thought we might be angels?"

Sarah-Jane rolled her eyes. "Yeah. How stupid was that?"

"Well, what *is* the difference between angels and fairies?"

"They are *so* different!" said Sarah-Jane.

"Are they?"

"Yes!" Rosie waved her fork excitedly. "Angels are boys, and fairies are girls."

Sarah-Jane shook her head. "No. Fairies *can* be boys."

Rosie's eyes widened. "Then can *Bert* be a fairy?"

Everyone looked at Rosie's plump old hippo, sitting at the end of the table.

"*Please*, Sarah-Jane?" begged Rosie. "*Please* can Bert be a fairy?"

"Well . . . I don't . . ." Sarah-Jane looked at Rosie's eager face. "OK. Bert can be a fairy."

"Wow, thanks, Sarah-Jane!"

Joe went on picking bits of onion out of his brown rice casserole.

Alice was still musing. "Maybe it's something to do with size. Aren't angels bigger than fairies? Or maybe it's the sort of wings—"

"I know!" cried Rosie suddenly. "I know what the difference is!"

Everyone looked at her.

"Angels are in winter and fairies are in summer!" cried Rosie. "Like football and cricket!"

If Joe hadn't been so fed up, he would have laughed . . .

Five

The next day they were still at it. In fact the girls wore their fairy outfits from the moment they got up. And Bert was transformed. Gone were the blue swimming-trunks he always wore. Instead his fat grey tummy had been forced into some sort of dress. And on his big round head was a circlet of tinsel. Most of the time he sat on top of the climbing frame (or "bower", as it now was.). He did not, Joe thought, look very happy.

Alice and Rosie, on the other hand, seemed happy. Most of the time. At one point Joe thought they looked a bit bored (Sarah-Jane had gone into the house for something). Tucking his baseball bat under one arm, he strolled towards them, throwing the ball in the air with a nice spin. He knew Rosie found it difficult to resist a game of baseball – particularly if he promised to give her easy pitches.

But before he could suggest a few throws, Sarah-Jane appeared from the house. "Alice! Rosie!" she called. The girls looked at her. "Come on!" said Sarah-Jane. "We have to plan the . . ." She glanced at Joe. "We have to plan

the you-know-what!"

"Oh. OK," said Alice. And followed
Sarah-Jane towards the climbing
frame.

Rosie gave him a regretful little
look, and followed the others.

Joe watched
as they disap-
peared into
the "bower".
And then
went in to
complain to
Mum.

Mum was
at her computer.

"I wouldn't mind them
being anything else!" Joe said.
"Like pirates. Or axe-murderers. Or
vampires. But . . . *fairies*!"

"Yes . . ." Mum clicked her mouse,
and looked at him. "It's difficult, I see

that. Maybe they'll get bored of it soon."

"They haven't yet!" said Joe.

"No . . ." agreed Mum. "They do seem very single-minded. Or rather, Sarah-Jane seems very single-minded." She frowned. "She's just been in here, actually. Came to have a word about something."

"What?" said Joe.

Mum sighed. "You'll find out soon enough."

Suddenly the doorbell rang. "Oh, good!" said Mum. "That will be Amanda! She's coming round to work on the computer for a bit." She peered at the screen, clicked her mouse again, and got up. "Now I can go round to the shops. Like to come, Joe?"

Joe looked at her. Walking to the shops with Mum? How much fun was that?

"I'll buy you a comic," said Mum.

"OK," said Joe.

Six

"Dad will be back at the weekend, remember," said Mum, as they walked along the road. "He said he might take you fishing."

"Cool!" Joe's heart rose. In fact the further Joe got from the fairy-infested garden, the better he felt. All right, the whole fairy thing was a pain. But Sarah-Jane was a guest, wasn't she? You were supposed to do what guests wanted. And maybe Mum was right about the girls getting bored soon . . .

They went to the little supermarket first. Mum grabbed a wire basket and went round getting the stuff she usually got, like fruit and carrots and wholemeal bread. Then – to Joe's amazement – she went to the biscuit and cake shelves and started filling her basket with packets.

He stared. This was *so* unlike Mum! Mum was mad about healthy eating. She even had healthy food at *parties*! Yet here she was buying coloured biscuits and pink wafers and little cakes! Sweet, sugary, sticky things – the sort she *never* bought!

"Wow, Mum!" said Joe. "All this good stuff you're buying. Thanks!"

Mum looked at her basket and made a face. "Come on, let's get this and go on to the newsagent!"

Just outside the newsagent's, Mum said, "Oh, no!" She put down one of her bags, and started smoothing her hair. "Mrs de Vere's in there! She always looks so elegant. And whenever I see her, I'm looking a *tip*!"

Joe looked through the shop window. Yes, Mrs de Vere was standing inside dressed in a grey-and-mauve dress, a shopping bag over her arm. Mrs de Vere lived in the next street along to theirs, but their gardens joined at the bottom. Apparently she had been a well-known actress when she was younger. The three young Campbells were a little scared of her.

"You look fine, Mum!" said Joe.

"Oh, well . . ." Mum pushed the door, and they both went in.

Mrs de Vere turned, and smiled when she saw Mum. "Hello, my dear!" she said in her ringing voice. "I'm *so* pleased to see you. I have been meaning to get in touch."

"Oh . . . yes?" said Mum.

Joe made for the magazine rack.

Maybe he could find a comic with a
good free gift . . .

"Yes, I need some help from your
gorgeous children!" said Mrs de Vere.

"Really?"

"You see, my daughter's child has
come to stay. For a week. And I know
so few young round here." She looked
at Mum. "I wondered if some of

yours might . . ."

"Oh, yes," said Mum. "I'm sure they would!"

Mrs de Vere smiled again. "How very, very kind . . ."

"Er . . . your grandchild . . . ?"

"Yes?" said Mrs de Vere.

"A girl or a . . . boy?"

Joe looked up from the magazine rack, waiting for her answer.

"Oh, a girl!" Joe's heart sank. *It would be a girl.*

"She's called Melpomene!"

She would have a silly name like Melpomene.

"She's a perfect poppet."

She would be a perfect poppet.

"Such a wonderful little ballerina!"

She would be a wonderful little ballerina.

And Joe made his decision then and there. He, Joe Campbell, wasn't going anywhere *near* Mrs de Vere's perfect poppet of a granddaughter with the stupid name!

Seven

"Of course we must help with Mrs de Vere's granddaughter!" said Mum as they walked back. "She says you can go through to her garden from the bottom of ours, rather than walking round."

Joe said nothing. He had made up his mind, and he wasn't going to change it. He would have nothing to do with Mrs de Vere's granddaughter. As he walked along, he pulled at the "free super-spinner" on the front of his magazine. He gave one last wrench and the "free super-spinner" came away – with a wing missing. It didn't look as

though it was going to do much spinning now. Joe shoved it into his pocket with a sigh.

When they got home they found Amanda in the kitchen, making herself some coffee.

"Hey!" She nodded towards the garden. "What's up with *that*?"

"Fairies!" Mum put her bags on the worktop. "Just our fairies!"

"Oh, I love the fairies!" said Amanda. "But what about that Sarah-Jane?"

"What do you mean?" Mum started to unpack, putting the cakes and biscuits in a pile.

"Well, I caught her taking your lacy white cushions into the garden, and tried to stop her."

"And?"

"I failed."

Mum laughed, and added some mini-marshmallows to the pile. "Well, thanks for trying."

Suddenly Amanda noticed all the sweets and biscuits. "Hey, what is this? I've never seen you buy anything like this!"

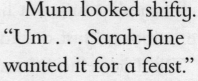

Mum looked shifty. "Um . . . Sarah-Jane wanted it for a feast."

"A feast?" said Joe. "I haven't heard about a feast!"

Mum drew a hand through her hair. "A fairy feast. Tomorrow, I think."

Amanda looked through some of the packets. "Well, if this is the sort of thing fairies like, I'm amazed they can fly! You'd think they'd be too fat to achieve lift-off!"

Mum gave a thin smile.

Joe looked at all the food Mum had bought for the feast – and made up his mind. He would just have to make sure no one could possibly see from the road . . .

He found Rosie kneeling on the grass, picking daisies. "About this fairy feast, Rosie . . ."

She looked up. "Yes?"

"Will you tell the others . . . OK, I'll *come* to the fairy feast. Except that I won't dress up."

Rosie got to her feet. "I'll go and talk to them."

She was only away a few seconds. "Sorry," she said, panting. "Sarah-Jane says 'No'."

"*No?*"

"No. Whether you dress up or not. It's no. You can't come to the feast."

41

Joe stared at Rosie. "But why not?"

"Because you might frighten them."

"Frighten who?"

"The fairies, of course!" And, before he could say anything else, Rosie ran off.

Joe stared after her. A feeling of fury flooded through him.

How dare they leave him out! He – Joe – who always had the best ideas for doing stuff! He turned angrily towards the house. Well, he had better have some ideas now – ideas for

things to do on his own. He took a couple of steps. And then he stopped. And did something that he had sworn he would never do. He walked down to the bottom of the lawn. Climbed through a straggly bit of hedge. Wriggled past the end of the fence. And into Mrs de Vere's garden . . .

Eight

Joe looked around the de Vere garden. It was bigger than the Campbell garden. The house was bigger too. And older . . .

There was no one in sight. Not Mrs de Vere. Not the "perfect poppet" granddaughter. No one. Slowly Joe walked up the garden towards the house. There was a paved area near the back door, with a little pond in the middle. He made for that. He could see an old swing-seat on the edge of the paved area but could not make out if someone was sitting in it. He felt too shy to shout something.

He looked around as he walked. On his left was an oblong piece of lawn with strange little archways arranged around it. What – or *who* –

were these archways for? He stared at them as he passed. Weren't they just the right size for . . . ? 'Stop it!' he told himself. Really, he was getting as bad as the girls! The archways were probably something to do with gardening . . .

Just then he came level with some big green bushes. There was a little rustle behind him, the sort that a bird or a cat might make. And then a voice rang through the summer air. A voice full of challenge. "*Freeze!*"

Joe had watched enough television. He froze.

"Stay right there!" ordered the voice. "I am armed, and I'm not afraid to use it!"

Joe did stay right there. His heart was hammering.

"Who are you?" demanded the voice. "And what are you

doing in this garden?"

"I'm . . . I'm Joe Campbell," said
Joe. "And Mrs de Vere said I could
come in."

There was a silence.

"Oh. OK." The voice sounded less
fierce now. "You can turn round now,
Joe Campbell. Slowly, mind!"

Joe did turn round. His eyes fell on
someone crouched on the ground,
right up against the nearest bush. The
someone was about his age. The
someone had a frown on its face. The
someone had, trained on him, a . . .

"That's not a gun!" said Joe. "It's a
stick!"

Nine

The person by the bushes got up. Joe now saw it was a girl. She wore blue dungarees, with one strap flapping loose. Her face and knees were dirty.

"I never said I did have a gun." The girl tossed back a brown plait. "I just said I was armed."

"A stick's not an arm!" said Joe. "I mean—"

"I know what you mean." The girl came forward a few steps. "But you still haven't told me what you're doing here!"

"Mrs de Vere said I could. I'm looking for her granddaughter. The one with a funny name, who's wonderful at ballet and a perfect poppet!"

The girl rolled her eyes.

Joe looked at her. "Do you know where she is?"

"Yes."

"Where?"

The girl shrugged. "Oh, let's not bother about her." She fastened her dungaree strap, and looked towards the pond. "Do you like sea battles?"

"*What?*"

"Sea battles! I've made all these

boats, and floated them on the pond. But I need someone to play against."

Joe looked over at the pond. Sure enough, there were some paper boats floating on the surface. "OK," he said.

Joe enjoyed the battle. The girl enjoyed the battle. The goldfish probably did not enjoy the battle, as they swam to the bottom until it was all over. Joe sank several of the girl's boats. And the girl sank several of his.

"Let's call it a draw!" she said, picking up a dripping boat which

had once been the pride of her fleet.

"OK!" said Joe, reaching out near a lily leaf for another.

They piled the ruined boats in a heap, and sat back on their heels. Joe wondered if he should leave now. He could say, "Great sea battle. Thanks. I'll be off now." He could – and perhaps he should. But he didn't want to.

The girl looked at him, eyebrows raised. He met her gaze. "Well, Joe," she said. "What would you like to do now?"

Joe's heart leaped. And then he realized that he ought to answer her question. What *would* he like to do now? He usually found this difficult to say at other people's houses. But this time he knew the answer. "I'd like to look at those archways."

"*What?*"

Joe nodded down the garden.

"Those little archways. On the lawn down there . . ."

The girl followed his gaze, then turned back to him. There was a twinkle in her eyes. For a moment Joe thought she was going to laugh at him. But she didn't. She said, "Those little archways . . ."

"Yes?"

"Are hoops."

"Yes?"

"For croquet."

Joe, who was good at most games, got the hang of croquet fairly quickly. He liked the "thwack" when his mallet hit a ball full on. The girl got to the winning post first, but he wasn't *that* far behind.

"Not bad," said the girl, picking up her ball. "Not bad at all for a first game."

Joe lowered his mallet behind his red ball – he wanted to finish his round, for practice. "Do you play much?"

"No," said the girl. "Not much. Only when I'm staying with Grandma."

Joe hit the red ball hard. *Thwack!* He watched it speed across the lawn, about a metre wide of the winning post. And suddenly he realized what the girl had said.

Ten

"*You* are the granddaughter!" cried Joe. "*You* are Mrs de Vere's granddaughter with the funny name who does ballet!"

The girl looked at him. "Well, come on!" she said. "Who did you *think* I was?"

"I just thought . . . you couldn't be . . ." Joe trailed off. He realized that he had *not* been clever. And he had also told the girl – twice – that she had a funny name. Perhaps he should just slink back home . . . He looked towards his garden. He couldn't see any fairies, but he knew they were there.

"Do you like climbing trees?" said the girl.

"What?"

"That one over there is good."

Joe followed her gaze to a large spreading tree.

"You can't go that high on it," she said. "But when you get up, the branches are wide and you can lie down on them."

Joe looked at the tree. Then he looked towards his own garden. Then he looked at the girl.

"OK!" he said.

He could always slink home later.

She was right about the tree. It was

easy to climb, and the branches were wide and flattish, so you could lie down on them. Joe lay back on his branch, and gazed at the ceiling of green leaves. He rubbed the tree bark with his foot. As he did so, he felt something in his trouser pocket.

Joe put in a hand and drew out something plastic. He stared at it and suddenly realized what it was. It was the "super-spinner" he had pulled off the magazine on the way back from the shops . . .

"What have you got there?" The girl was one branch above.

"Nothing," said Joe.

"Go on. What is it?"

"It's a super-spinner with a wing missing," said Joe.

"Does it work?"

"I don't know."

"Try."

Joe threw the spinner into the air. Both watched as it fell like a stone to the ground below. They looked at each other – and burst out laughing.

"About your name . . ." said Joe, picking with his nails at the tree bark.

"Yes?"

"Well . . . I'm sorry I said it was funny."

The girl laughed. "Oh, don't worry! It *is* a bit funny. Hardly anyone but

Grandma calls me Melpomene, any-way."

"What do they call you, then?"

"Mel."

"Mel . . ." he repeated.

They were silent for a bit.

Then Joe spoke. "So what's it like staying with your grandma?" He didn't say he thought Mrs de Vere was scary.

"Actually she's cool!" said Mel. "Different. She says poetry when we do the washing-up." Mel made her voice all deep. "*For he on honey-dew hath fed, And drunk the milk of Paradise!*"

"Yes." Joe could imagine Mrs de Vere doing that. "Was she really a well-known actress?"

"She was! And so's my mother. An actress, I mean. Though not so well-known." Mel sat up and started climbing down the tree. "She's working in a film now. That's why I'm here."

"Wow!" Joe turned over, and started feeling for a foothold beneath him.

"It's not wow at all, really!" Mel moved nimbly down. "I don't see why everyone's so impressed by acting. Take Grandma. Spent all her life in the theatre and still mad about it." She landed lightly on the ground.

"Really?" Joe landed (more heavily) in front of her.

"Yup. She keeps all this theatre stuff around. Costumes and playbills and things. She has the first costume Mum ever wore in a real play. It fits me, actually."

"What is it?"

"Cobweb."

Joe started laughing. "A cobweb? What sort of a part is that?"

"Not *a* cobweb. *Cobweb!*"

"*What?*"

"A fairy!"

Joe stopped laughing.

"Why are you looking all cross like that?" said Mel.

"You don't really want to know," said Joe.

"I do," said Mel.

"You don't," said Joe.

"I do," said Mel.

So he told her everything, from the minute Sarah-Jane had arrived. He even told her about the assault course.

Mel listened. She thought the

assault course sounded really good.
She did not laugh at him for having
fairies in his garden. And she was
most indignant about the feast. "How
mean! I don't have a brother, but if I
did, I would definitely invite him to
my fairy feast!"

"Melpomene!" a voice called.

It was Mrs de Vere, standing by the
back door.

"Oh, there's Grandma!" Mel turned back to Joe. "I'd better go in. She probably wants to know what I want for supper."

"Yes," said Joe. "It'll be about our tea time too."

"See you, then!" said Mel lightly.

"See you!" said Joe.

And he walked down to the fence and wriggled through to his own garden.

Eleven

Mum turned round from the cooker as he went into the kitchen. "Ah, there you are!" she said. "Tea's ready!"

"I've just met the granddaughter!" said Joe.

"What? The one with the funny name?" Mum shot him a look. "What's she like?"

"She's *OK*, actually. And hardly anyone calls her by her funny name. Most people call her Mel."

Suddenly they heard the girls' voices as they came towards the kitchen.

"Don't say anything about Mel to the girls yet, will you, Mum?" Joe begged, lowering his voice.

Mum met his eye, and shook her

head, just as the girls came in . . .

"About this feast tomorrow," said Joe, as everyone was eating their yoghurt and honey.

"Yes?" Sarah-Jane had a guarded look.

"Well, Rosie said something about . . . having real fairies."

"Yes!" cried Rosie. "We wrote lovely invitations on bark, and put them round the garden. Three o'clock tomorr—!"

"Be quiet, Rosie!" hissed Sarah-Jane.

Rosie looked guilty. Then she looked at her hippo. "Be quiet, Bert!" she said (which wasn't really fair, as Bert hadn't said anything).

"But . . ." Joe looked at Sarah-Jane. "*Surely* you don't believe in fairies?"

Sarah-Jane shrugged. "Some grown-ups believe in fairies. It says so in my book. And lots of people believe in angels and things . . ."

Joe looked at Alice. Alice did not meet his eye. Then he looked at Mum. "Mum! Tell them there's no such thing as fairies!"

Mum who was stacking things in the dishwasher, laughed. "Who knows, Joe?"

Joe slammed his spoon down. Had the world gone mad? "I know! *I* know there's no such thing as fairies!"

Later he found Mum reading a newspaper in the front room. "Why didn't you tell them, Mum?" he demanded.

"Tell them what?" said Mum.

"About there being no fairies!"

Mum frowned. "Well, in a way Sarah-Jane is right."

"*What?*"

"People do believe in the most extraordinary things." Mum glanced at her paper and sighed. "You only have to read the news to know that."

"But . . . *you* know there's no such thing as fairies."

"Yes," said Mum. "But I can't prove it. No one can prove it."

Joe crossed his arms over his chest. "When I grow up, I'm going to be a scientist. And I will *prove* that fairies don't exist!"

Mum smiled. "Good on you, Joe," she said. "In the meantime, let the girls have their fun." She laughed. "And maybe we're wrong. Maybe a fairy *will* turn up at their blessed feast!"

And that was when Joe had his idea . . .

Twelve

The next day was sunny. The birds sang. The bees buzzed. The fairies flitted. Sarah-Jane, Alice and Rosie were preparing for their feast.

At first they spread the white table-cloth under the climbing frame. But later they changed their minds, and moved it down the garden, to a spot under the apple-tree. They scattered

petals over it and picked leaves from the bushes to arrange the food on. They spent a lot of time discussing what to wear. And what to drink. And what time they should make the mini-sandwiches.

Bert was washed and dried so that his "fur" looked nice.

Joe visited Mel in the morning – but then came home. He thought he might tidy his room, and then thought that he might not. But he spent a happy few hours playing computer games and reading magazines.

A few minutes before 3 p.m., Joe closed the magazine he was reading and threw it under his bed. Then he walked downstairs into the garden and hoisted himself up onto the climbing frame. From there he had a good view of the scene under the apple-tree. The feast, he had to admit to himself, did look good.

"Take no notice," he heard Sarah-Jane say. "He just wants to be invited."

Rosie looked at him. "Couldn't—?" she started, but then she stopped.

Alice seemed rather quiet (she had lost the argument about when to make the mini-sandwiches).

Joe looked at his watch. Five seconds to three.

Sarah-Jane put a CD into her CD-player, and pressed a button. Silvery music floated out into the summer air. That really was a good touch, thought Joe admiringly. You had to hand it to Sa—

And then his heart skipped a beat.

Thirteen

The fairy was amazing. Even though Joe was expecting her, he was amazed. She appeared suddenly from nowhere, sweeping round the apple-tree in perfect time to the music. She was dressed in something shimmery and floaty and magical that was all sorts of colours at once. Her long brown hair was loose and crinkly, her face had a strange *greenish* glow. Staring at her, Joe realized – to his surprise – that she was beautiful. The fairy slowed her steps as she approached the feast, then folded herself gracefully into a sitting position in front of the tablecloth.

If Joe was amazed, the girls were thunderstruck. They just sat stock-still, gazing at her. Alice's mouth was wide

open. Rosie's face had gone bright red. Sarah-Jane – Sarah-Jane just stared at the vision before her.

What do you do if you invite a fairy to your fairy feast – and a fairy comes?

Joe went up to the tablecloth and knelt down beside Rosie. No one even looked at him. Everyone seemed to expect Sarah-Jane to take the lead. But she did nothing.

Alice was the one to act. She picked up a leaf-plate of mini-sandwiches and, with slightly shaking hands, offered them to the fairy.

The fairy stared at them, but didn't move. Then she spoke, a strange high sound against the music. "Honey-dew . . . ?"

The girls stared at the feast spread in front of them. So magical once, it now seemed to have lost its magic. (The mini-sandwiches were already

curling in the sun.) Honey-dew? No.
No honey-dew. Alice shook her head.

Sarah-Jane still did nothing.

Rosie picked up the little crystal
jug and offered it. "Apple juice?" she
said.

The fairy stared at the jug, and
looked at Rosie. "Milk of paradise?"
she whispered.

The girls looked again at their
feast. No, there was definitely no milk
of paradise there. Rosie put the jug
down.

No one said anything for a few

seconds. Time seemed to stand still. The silvery music played on.

Then suddenly, in one smooth movement, the fairy rose to her feet. Her eyes swept over them all. She raised her (greenish) arms as if to say, "Farewell!"

Then she turned her beautiful head, stepped away behind the apple-tree – and was gone.

Fourteen

It was a long time before anyone said anything. Then Alice spoke in an awed voice. "Wow! That was . . . *Wow!*"

"She was so . . ." said Rosie.

"*Beautiful*," said Alice.

"Her hair," said Rosie.

"Her face," said Alice.

"Her clothes," said Rosie.

"Her hands," said Alice.

"Her feet," said Rosie.

"*Everything*," said Alice.

"A real fairy . . ." breathed Rosie. She looked indignantly at Joe. "And you said there was no such thing!"

There was silence.

Joe took a deep breath. "There isn't," he said.

"What do you mean?" said Sarah-Jane.

"It wasn't," said Joe.

"It wasn't a fairy?" said Sarah-Jane.

"No," said Joe.

"Well, what was it then?" said Alice.

Joe drew another breath. His heart was beating fast. But he had to say it. "It was a friend of mine. Her name is Mel."

Slowly he met Sarah-Jane's eye. He did not know what he would see in her pale face. Fury? Contempt? Hatred? What he did see surprised him. There was anger there, certainly. But there was also . . . relief.

Suddenly Alice gave a long drawn-out sigh. "We'll never look as good as that."

"No," said Rosie.

"Our costumes are nothing like hers!"

"No," said Rosie.

"And we never even *thought* of going green!" said Alice.

"No," said Rosie.

The sisters looked at each other.

"We've done a *lot* of fairies!" said Rosie.

"We have," said Alice.

"And there's not much you can do as a fairy. Not really."

"No," said Alice. She looked at Sarah-Jane, and then back at Rosie. "Let's have the feast, and then go and get changed."

Rosie nodded. Then she looked at Sarah-Jane. "Joe can stay for the feast, can't he? Now there's no fairies for him to frighten!"

There was a moment's silence.

Then Sarah-Jane pulled the tiara from her head, and slowly shook her hair out. "Yes . . ." she said. "Oh, yes . . ."

Rosie looked down at her hippo and tutted. "Do sit up, Bert!"

Bert was made to sit up.

Alice poured apple juice for everyone.

Joe crammed a little pink cake into his mouth and reached out for a handful of marshmallows . . .

Fifteen

The next morning Joe invited Mel to the Campbells' garden. She was wearing jeans and a T-shirt, and looked a bit shy.

If she was shy, Rosie was even shyer. "Was it really you?" she whispered.

"Yes," Mel whispered back.

Rosie hoisted Bert (now back in his blue swimming-trunks) up in her arms. "Bert thought you looked very nice," she said.

Mel looked at him. "Thank you, Bert," she said.

Just then Alice and Sarah-Jane came up. There was something a little awkward about both of them. And suddenly Joe didn't want to talk about fairies any more. That was all over now. "Meet Mel!" he said with a sweep of his hand. "And this is Alice and Sarah-Jane! What do you all say to a game of baseball?"

They all said yes.

"No!" shouted Joe. "You don't drop the bat when you run. You hang onto it!"

"Sorry, Joe!" Sarah-Jane made a face, and ran back for the bat. "I keep forgetting!"

"Never mind," said Joe kindly. "You're actually hitting quite well."

Mel came running up with the ball. "Can I pitch now?"

"OK," said Joe. He walked backwards a few paces, and took up position near the climbing frame (where Bert sat, watching the action).

Alice was still fielding, but Rosie had got bored, and was looking under the hedge for beetles (she said she wanted to make a beetle farm).

Mel tried a few pitches, but was sending them very wide, which was hard work for Alice.

"Can't we do something else?"
Alice looked hopefully at Mel. "Like
go into your garden?"

"OK," said Mel. "But we mustn't
make so much noise as last time.
Grandma said it was worse than the
battle scenes in *Henry the Fifth*!"

"All right – we promise!" said
Alice. And the six of them (hippo
included) swarmed down the garden.

Mel was first through, and ran on
ahead. Sarah-Jane followed, and Joe
waited as Alice helped Rosie and Bert
through the hedge. He walked up the

de Vere garden, past the croquet lawn, past the bushes where he had first met Mel. It felt so long ago now. So much had changed since then. Since the feast, no one had so much as mentioned fairies.

He smiled to himself.

Sixteen

It was weeks later.

Mel was long gone back to her mother's, Sarah-Jane to her parents'. Everyone was back at school.

Joe was out with Mum. He was just posting a letter in the box outside the post office, when Mrs de Vere suddenly appeared at his side.

"Oh, *hello*!" she said in her rich voice. "Aren't you one of those dear lovely Campbell children? The ones who played so nicely with Melpomene over the summer?"

"Yes," said Joe. It seemed the easiest thing to say.

Mrs de Vere turned to Mum as she came up. "They really were wonderful!" she said. "Such lively children!"

"Yes, they are quite . . . lively," said Mum.

"And, my dear, I'm so grateful about that fancy dress party you gave!"

Mum looked puzzled. "The what?"

"The fancy dress party! You must remember! Melpomene dressed up in Laura's old costume from *Midsummer Night's Dream*."

"Ah, fairies!" said Mum, her brow clearing. "Yes, there were a lot of fairies around at one point. That I do remember!"

"It was such fun!" said Mrs de Vere. "I helped Melpomene with the make-up and she looked a picture, though I say so myself!"

"I'm sure!" said Mum politely. "She's a good-looking girl."

"And talking of pictures," said Mrs de Vere, "I took some photographs of her in costume sitting in the old cedar, and they came out *beautifully*. I'm using them for my Christmas card this year!"

"What a good idea!" Mum glanced at her watch.

"I'm so grateful to you! And wondered if you'd like a photograph too." She smiled. "To remind you of your fancy dress party?"

Mum drew a breath. "Well, I don't want to put you to any trouble, Mrs de Vere—"

But Joe interrupted her. "Yes!"

They turned to him. Mum looked startled.

"I *would* like a picture of Mel in her fairy costume!" said Joe. He wanted that photo, and he wasn't going to pretend he didn't.

Mrs de Vere smiled at him.

Mum still looked puzzled. "I thought you couldn't stand fairies!"

"I can't!" said Joe.

"So . . . why . . . ?" said Mum.

He looked at her. "Mel's not a fairy, Mum. There's no such thing as fairies!"

THE END

ASTRID, THE AU PAIR FROM OUTER SPACE

Emily Smith

*Imagine being looked after by an alien
from outer space . . .*

When Harry's mum says they're getting an
'au pair' from another country, he's not quite
sure what to expect. When Astrid, who lives
on a planet 500 light years away, decides to
work as an 'au pair' on Earth, she's not
quite sure what to expect.

What Harry definitely doesn't expect is a girl
whose suitcase moves on its own, whose hair
sticks out like a dandelion clock and who
doesn't know what football is.

And Astrid is very surprised to find that
Harry's family has a special gadget for opening
tins and that his little brother Fred isn't a girl.

SMARTIES SILVER MEDAL WINNER

ISBN 0 552 54616 X

PATRICK THE PARTY-HATER

Emily Smith

Balloons? Sausages on sticks?
An entertainer? Oh NO!
It must be a party . . .

Patrick loves making models and creating
his own inventions. He does not love
Musical Bumps, big crowds and having
to be jolly. But his mum is convinced that
going to parties is good for him. She
even wants him to have one of his own.
Surely there must be a better idea?

A very special story from
a prize-winning author.

ISBN 0 552 55173 2

THE SHRIMP

Emily Smith

Wild life!

Ben spends the holidays with his nose in the sand and bottom in the air. It's not because he's shy – though some of his classmates do call him the Shrimp. It's because he's got a great idea for a wildlife project.

A competition is on! The class projects are going to be judged by a famous TV wildlife presenter, and the prize is irresistible. Ben would love to win it, but others have their eyes on the prize too . . .

SMARTIES GOLD MEDAL WINNER

ISBN 0 552 54735 2